States

OKLAHOMA

by Tyler Maine

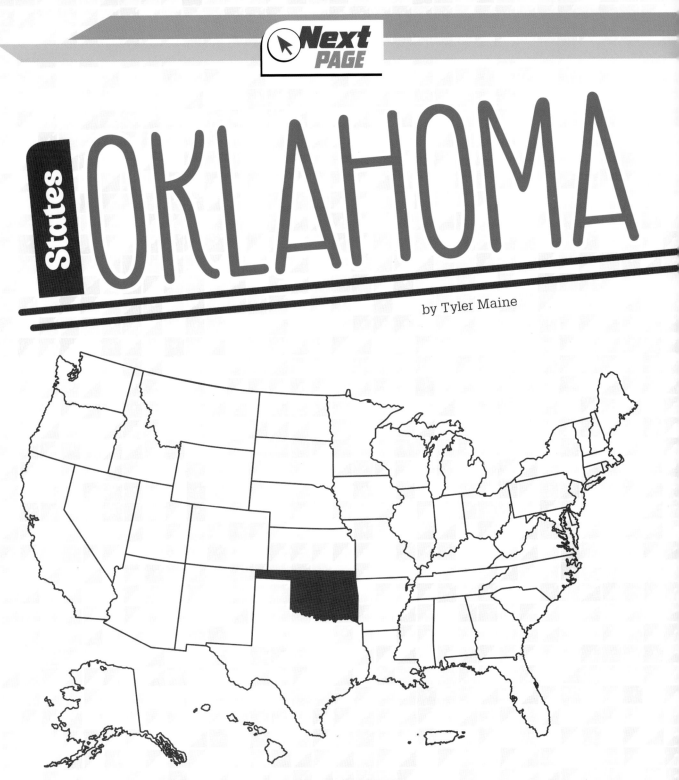

CAPSTONE PRESS
a capstone imprint

Next Page Books are published by Capstone Press,
1710 Roe Crest Drive, North Mankato, Minnesota 56003
www.mycapstone.com

Library of Congress Cataloging-in-Publication Data
Cataloging-in-publication information is on file with the Library of
Congress.
ISBN 978-1-5157-0423-2 (library binding)
ISBN 978-1-5157-0482-9 (paperback)
ISBN 978-1-5157-0534-5 (ebook PDF)

Editorial Credits
Jaclyn Jaycox, editor; Kazuko Collins and Katy LaVigne, designers;
Morgan Walters, media researcher; Tori Abraham, production specialist

Photo Credits
Alamy: 19th era, 25; Capstone Press: Angi Gahler, map 4, 7; Corbis:
Bettmann, top 19; CriaImages.com: Jay Robert Nash Collection, top 18;
Getty Images: Entertainment/Bob Berg, bottom 19, Getty Images Sport/
Sports Studio Photos, middle 19, Marilyn Angel Wynn, 10; Library
of Congress: Prints and Photographs Division Washington, D.C., 26;
Newscom: Album/M.G.M., middle 18, J.P. Wilson/Icon Sportswire
320/J.P. Wilson/Icon Sportswire, bottom 24, Julien McRoberts Danita
Delimont Photography, 11, Picture History, 12; North Wind Picture
Archives, 27; One Mile Up, Inc., flag, seal 23; Shutterstock: Brad
Whitsitt, 9, Daniel Prudek, bottom left 21, Henryk Sadura, 5, Jeff
Banke, top left 21, John A Davis, 7, Karin Hildebrand Lau, 16, Lustra,
14, Marina Kurrle, 6, bottom left 8, Minerva Studio, 29, Nancy
Bauer, top right 21, Natalia Bratslavsky, 13, Rusty Dodson, bottom
left 20, s_bukley, bottom 18, Sarah Cates, bottom right 21, Sarah
Jessup, top left 20, Shane Wilson Link, 15, Steve Byland, middle
right 21, Todd Shoemake, bottom right 8, tome213, middle left 21,
TwilightArtPictures, top right 20, val lawless, 17, Zeljko Radojko, cover,
Zorandim, top 24; U.S. Fish & Wildlife Service: Duane Raver, bottom
right 20; Wikimedia: FEMA News Photo, 28

All design elements by Shutterstock

Printed and bound in China.
0316/CA21600187
012016   009436F16

TABLE OF CONTENTS

Want to take your research further? Ask your librarian if your school subscribes to PebbleGo Next. If so, when you see this helpful symbol ⓚ throughout the book, log onto www.pebblegonext.com for bonus downloads and information.

LOCATION

Oklahoma is located in the south-central United States. Oklahoma is shaped like a cooking pan. A thin strip of land sticks out toward the west. That's the Panhandle. Kansas and Colorado are north of Oklahoma. Arkansas and Missouri are on the east. To the south and west is Texas. New Mexico lies west of the Panhandle. Oklahoma City, the capital, is the state's largest city. Tulsa and Norman are the state's next largest cities.

PebbleGo Next Bonus!
To print and label your own map, go to www.pebblegonext.com and search keywords:
OK MAP

Legend
- ✪ Capital
- ● City
- ～ River

Scale
Miles
0   25   50   75   100
0   25   50   75   100
Kilometers

COLORADO
NEW MEXICO
KANSAS
MISSOURI
ARKANSAS

OKLAHOMA
Bartlesville
Stillwater ●   Tulsa ●   Broken Arrow
Edmond ●   Muskogee
Oklahoma City ✪ ● Midwest City
Norman ●
Lawton ●

Red River

TEXAS

Oklahoma City is one of only two capital cities where the state name is part of the city name.

GEOGRAPHY

The Interior Plains cover northern Oklahoma. Northwestern Oklahoma is covered in grasslands. Oklahoma's highest point at 4,973 feet (1,516 meters), Black Mesa, is in the Panhandle. The Ouachita Mountains are part of the Interior Highlands, which cover eastern Oklahoma. The Coastal Plains region is located along the Oklahoma-Texas border. The Coastal Plains is part of the Gulf Coastal Plains region that spreads north from the Gulf of Mexico. The region consists of hills, swamplands, and rolling prairies.

PebbleGo Next Bonus! To watch a video about the Cherokee Indians, go to www.pebblegonext.com and search keywords:

OK VIDEO

There are more than 130 species of trees native to Oklahoma.

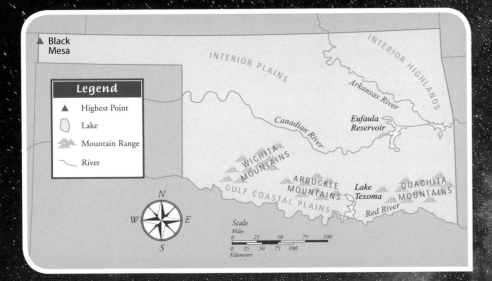

Black Mesa

Legend
▲ Highest Point
Lake
Mountain Range
River

INTERIOR PLAINS

INTERIOR HIGHLANDS

Arkansas River

Canadian River

Eufaula Reservoir

WICHITA MOUNTAINS

ARBUCKLE MOUNTAINS

Lake Texoma

OUACHITA MOUNTAINS

GULF COASTAL PLAINS

Red River

N W E S

Scale
Miles
0 25 50 75 100
0 25 50 75 100
Kilometers

In addition to being the highest point, Black Mesa is also the driest and coldest place in Oklahoma.

WEATHER

Winter temperatures in Oklahoma vary across the state. In winter northwestern Oklahoma is cooler than the southeast. The average winter temperature in Oklahoma is 39 degrees Fahrenheit (4 degrees Celsius). Summers are long and hot across the state. The state's average summer temperature is 80°F (27°C).

Average High and Low Temperatures (Oklahoma City, OK)

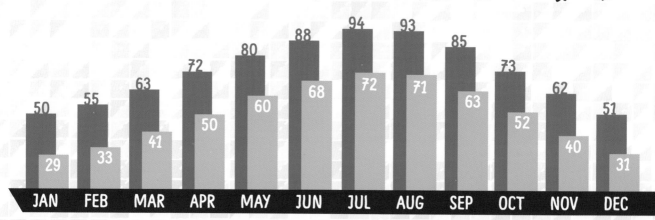

JAN	FEB	MAR	APR	MAY	JUN	JUL	AUG	SEP	OCT	NOV	DEC
50	55	63	72	80	88	94	93	85	73	62	51
29	33	41	50	60	68	72	71	63	52	40	31

Oklahoma City National Memorial

This memorial and museum honors those affected by the 1995 bombing. The museum tells visitors the story of this historical event.

Cherokee National Museum

This museum in Park Hill teaches visitors about Cherokee heritage. It includes a permanent exhibit on the Indian journey called the Trail of Tears.

Oklahoma Route 66 Museum

During the Great Depression (1929–1939), many Americans moved west to find work. Many traveled along Route 66. Galleries at this museum show visitors what it was like to travel along this road. The museum also gives visitors an idea of what America was like in the 1940s and 1950s.

HISTORY AND GOVERNMENT

President Andrew Jackson forced the Cherokee to move to Oklahoma from their land east of the Mississippi River.

In the early 1800s the United States was expanding to the west. White settlers wanted to claim American Indian land. In the 1820s the government began moving Indians to Indian Territory—today's eastern Oklahoma. Thousands of Indians died from disease and hunger during the journey. The Cherokee call this horrible experience the Trail of Tears.

After the Civil War (1861–1865), the U.S. government opened land in Indian Territory for white settlement. In 1889 oil was discovered near Tulsa. Oklahoma quickly became the place to strike it rich. On November 16, 1907, Oklahoma, including Indian Territory, became the 46th state.

Oklahoma's state government has three branches. The legislative branch makes the state laws. It has a 48-member Senate and a 101-member House of Representatives. The executive branch carries out laws. It is led by the governor. The judicial branch is made up of judges and courts. They uphold the laws.

Oklahoma's state capitol is surrounded by working oil wells.

INDUSTRY

Oklahoma's economy includes a range of industries, including service and manufacturing. Machinery and electrical equipment are Oklahoma's top manufactured products. An automobile assembly plant is located in Oklahoma City. Other factories make tires and electronics.

Oklahoma is a leading producer of natural gas and petroleum. The state is also rich in other natural resources. Coal, limestone, salt, gypsum, and iodine are mined in Oklahoma. Oklahoma is the only state that produces iodine. This chemical is used in medicine and added to salt.

Winter wheat is a main ingredient in many pastas, breads, biscuits, and crackers.

About 75 percent of Oklahoma's land is used to graze cattle or grow crops. Beef from cattle is the leading farm product. Poultry and hogs are also raised in Oklahoma. Winter wheat is Oklahoma's leading farm crop.

Oklahoma is one of the nation's top sources of beef.

POPULATION

Most Oklahomans have European backgrounds. Many are of German, Irish, and English descent. Others have descendants from Poland, Russia, Italy, Greece, Scotland, Wales, and the former Czechoslovakia. Immigrants came to Oklahoma when land was opened for settlement and during the mining boom.

About 7 percent of Oklahomans are American Indians. Oklahoma has more American Indian–owned land than any other state. Most of the Hispanic Americans in Oklahoma have Mexican backgrounds. Most African-Americans in the state live in Oklahoma City and Tulsa. Some live in small towns such as Langston. Langston was founded in 1889 as a completely African-American town.

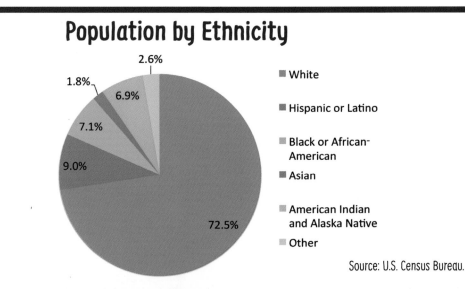

Population by Ethnicity

- 2.6%
- 1.8%
- 6.9%
- 7.1%
- 9.0%
- 72.5%

- White
- Hispanic or Latino
- Black or African-American
- Asian
- American Indian and Alaska Native
- Other

Source: U.S. Census Bureau.

FAMOUS PEOPLE

Jim Thorpe (1887–1953) was a track-and-field sports star. He won two gold medals in the 1912 Olympic Games. He was also a professional football and baseball player. He was born in Prague, Oklahoma.

Maria Tallchief (1925–2013) was a world-class ballerina. She danced with the New York City Ballet and founded the Chicago City Ballet. She was born in Fairfax.

Carrie Underwood (1983–) is an award-winning country music singer. She grew up on a farm in Checotah.

Will Rogers (1879–1935) was a comedian and a stage and movie actor. He was called the Cherokee Cowboy. He was born in Oologah.

Mickey Mantle (1931–1995) was a star baseball player for the New York Yankees. He was born in Spavinaw.

Mary Pope Osborne (1949–) is a children's book writer best known for the Magic Tree House series. She was born in Fort Sill.

STATE SYMBOLS

Tree

redbud

Flower

mistletoe

Bird

scissor-tailed flycatcher

Fish

white bass

PebbleGo Next Bonus! To make a popular Oklahoma dish, go to www.pebblegonext.com and search keywords:

OK RECIPE

Game Bird

wild turkey

Rock

rose rock

Wildflower

Indian blanket

Animal

bison, or American buffalo

Insect

honeybee

Butterfly

black swallowtail

FAST FACTS

STATEHOOD
1907

CAPITAL ☆
Oklahoma City

LARGEST CITY •
Oklahoma City

SIZE
68,595 square miles (177,660 square kilometers) land area (2010 U.S. Census Bureau)

POPULATION
3,850,568 (2013 U.S. Census estimate)

STATE NICKNAME
Sooner State

STATE MOTTO
"Labor Omnia Vincit," which is Latin for "Labor Conquers All Things"

STATE SEAL

Oklahoma's state seal has one large star. The star displays symbols of the Five Civilized Tribes, which first settled the region. The seal also displays an American Indian and a white frontiersman shaking hands before the figure of justice. This interaction shows how the people of Oklahoma got along with each other. The seal was adopted in 1907.

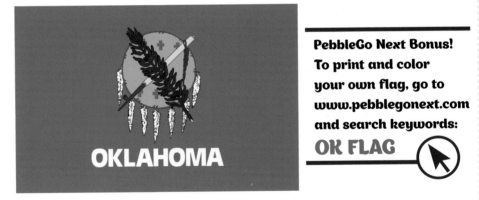

PebbleGo Next Bonus!
To print and color your own flag, go to www.pebblegonext.com and search keywords:
OK FLAG

STATE FLAG

The state flag is blue with an Osage warrior's shield in the center. The shield is decorated with seven eagle feathers to represent strength. Small crosses on the face of the shield represent the American Indian symbol for the stars in the sky. An olive branch and a peace pipe cross the shield. They stand for peace. The flag was adopted in 1925.

MINING PRODUCTS
natural gas, petroleum, limestone

MANUFACTURED GOODS
machinery, petroleum and coal products, fabricated metal, food products

FARM PRODUCTS
beef cattle, wheat

PROFESSIONAL SPORTS TEAMS
Oklahoma City Thunder (NBA)
Tulsa Shock (WNBA)

PebbleGo Next Bonus!
To learn the lyrics to the state song, go to www.pebblegonext.com and search keywords:
OK SONG

OKLAHOMA TIMELINE

1450
The Spiro mound builders have left Oklahoma; other American Indians move into the area.

1541
Francisco Vasquez de Coronado explores Oklahoma in search of gold.

1620
The Pilgrims establish a colony in the New World in present-day Massachusetts.

1682
French explorer René Robert Cavelier, known as Sieur de la Salle, claims Oklahoma for France.

1803 The United States buys the Oklahoma region from France as part of the Louisiana Purchase.

1828 The U.S. government establishes Oklahoma as Indian Territory.

1830–1842 The Five Civilized Tribes are forced to move to Oklahoma on what came to be called the Trail of Tears.

1861–1865 The Union and the Confederacy fight the Civil War. Most Indian tribes in Indian Territory fight for the Confederacy, but some align with the Union.

1889 Oil is discovered near Tulsa, bringing more people to Oklahoma hoping to strike it rich.

 **1889** On April 22 the United States opens part of Oklahoma to white settlement.

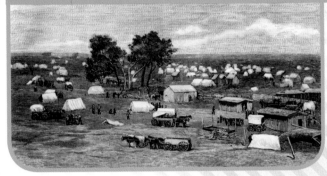

 **1890** U.S. Congress establishes Oklahoma Territory; the Panhandle is added to the state.

 **1907** Oklahoma becomes the 46th state on November 16.

 **1914–1918** World War I is fought; the United States enters the war in 1917.

1929–1939 The Great Depression and drought cause many Oklahomans to leave the state in search of jobs.

1939–1945 World War II is fought; the United States enters the war in 1941.

1982 Oklahoma's economy suffers as world oil prices drop.

1995 A bomb is set off on April 19 in front of the Alfred P. Murrah Federal Building in Oklahoma City, killing 168 people.

 **2001** On February 19 the Oklahoma City National Memorial Museum opens to honor the people killed in the 1995 bombing.

 **2013** On May 20 a tornado causes $2 billion in damage in Moore, just south of Oklahoma City.

 **2015** Oklahoma City has its first ever flash flood emergency in May.

Glossary

bomb *(BOM)*—a set of explosives or a holder filled with explosives

descend *(dee-SEND)*—if you are descended from someone, you belong to a later generation of the same family

drought *(DROUT)*—a long period of weather with little or no rainfall

executive *(ig-ZE-kyuh-tiv)*—the branch of government that makes sure laws are followed

expand *(ik-SPAND)*—to grow larger

heritage *(HER-uh-tij)*—the culture and traditions of one's family, ancestors, or country

immigrant *(IM-uh-gruhnt)*—someone who comes from abroad to live permanently in a country

industry *(IN-duh-stree)*—a business which produces a product or provides a service

judicial *(joo-DISH-uhl)*—to do with the branch of government that explains and interprets the laws

legislature *(LEJ-iss-lay-chur)*—a group of elected officials who have the power to make or change laws for a country or state

petroleum *(puh-TROH-lee-uhm)*—an oily liquid found below the earth's surface used to make gasoline, heating oil, and many other products

Read More

Dillard, Sheri. *What's Great About Oklahoma?* Our Great States. Minneapolis: Lerner Publications Company, 2015.

Ganeri, Anita. *United States of America: A Benjamin Blog and His Inquisitive Dog Guide.* Country Guides. Chicago: Heinemann Raintree, 2015.

Sanders, Doug. *Oklahoma.* It's My State! New York: Marshall Cavendish Benchmark, 2014.

Internet Sites

FactHound offers a safe, fun way to find Internet sites related to this book. All of the sites on FactHound have been researched by our staff.

Here's all you do:

Visit *www.facthound.com*

Type in this code: 9781515704232

Super-cool stuff!

Check out projects, games and lots more at
www.capstonekids.com

Critical Thinking Using the Common Core

1. Describe the shape of the state of Oklahoma. (Key Ideas and Details)

2. Look at the map on page 7. What river runs along the southern border of Oklahoma? (Craft and Structure)

3. Oklahoma is a leading producer of natural gas and petroleum. What is petroleum? (Craft and Structure)

Index